Martha Just Wants to Know!

Written and Illustrated by

Kimberly Hallinan

ISBN 979-8-89428-264-0 (paperback)
ISBN 979-8-89428-265-7 (hardcover)
ISBN 979-8-89428-266-4 (digital)

Christian Faith Publishing
832 Park Avenue
Meadville, PA 16335
www.christianfaithpublishing.com

Printed in the United States of America

Martha Just Wants to Know!

To all "my kids" whoever came through my classroom—I am so proud of you!

Meet Martha, a monkey as curious as can be,
asking so many questions,
as you will soon see.

In Africa, she has many friends,
which means that her questions will never end.

Asking questions she enjoyed.
But will the other animals become annoyed?

On *Sunday*, Martha came across a zebra eating grass
in the sun.
When a question bubbled up, she thought,
Won't this be fun?
She said, "Hello! It's the beginning of the week,
and I am hoping YOU can give me the answer that I
seek...
Why do you have stripes?"

The zebra replied with a smile,
"You know that we travel in groups called a zeal.
My stripes help me camouflage so I will not become the
next meal!"

"Thank you!" said Martha. "You have taught me a lot
and gave me the answer that I have sought!
Toodle-looooo!
Have fun hiding!"

On *Monday*, Martha stumbled upon a lion ready to pounce
on prey.
When a question bubbled up, she thought,
I'll ask quietly, in a special way.
She whispered, "Hello! It's the second day of the week,
and I am hoping YOU can give me the answer that I
seek...
Why do you roar so loud?"

The lion growled his reply,
"I only have an hour...
I use my ferocious roar to show my mighty power!"
Martha was scared.

"Thank you!" said Martha. "You have taught me a lot
and gave me the answer that I have sought!
Toodle-looooo!
Have fun hunting!"

On *Tuesday*, Martha discovered a giraffe eating lunch on an acacia tree.
When a question bubbled up, she thought,
Surely SHE will talk to me!
She said, "Hello! It's the third day of the week,
and I am hoping YOU can give me the answer that I seek…
Why is your neck so long?"

The giraffe answered sweetly,
"It is so I can eat my favorite food.
Eating lots of acacia leaves puts me in a really great mood!"

"Thank you!" said Martha. "You have taught me a lot
and gave me the answer that I have sought!
Toodle-looooo!
Have fun munching!"

On *Wednesday*, Martha bumped into a gorilla resting in
the shade.
When a question bubbled up, she thought,
I will ask and not be afraid.
She said, "Hello! It's the middle of the week,
and I am hoping YOU can give me the answer that I
seek...
Why do you beat your chest?"

The gorilla opened one eye and said,
"It is because when I do, I will not fail
to get the attention and love of a female."

"Thank you!" said Martha "You have taught me a lot
and gave me the answer that I have sought!
Toodle-looooo!
Have fun napping!"

On *Thursday*, Martha caught sight of a crocodile
  taking a swim down in the Nile.
When a question bubbled up, she thought,
I think my question might make him smile.
She said, "Hello! It's almost the end of the week,
and I am hoping YOU can give me the answer that I
seek...
Why do you STILL have so many teeth?"

With his toothy grin, the croc replied,
"Haven't you heard the news?
I can grow back every tooth that I lose!"

"Thank you!" said Martha. "You have taught me a lot
and gave me the answer that I have sought!
Toodle-looooo!
Have fun chomping!"

Across Africa word had spread
that Martha had too many questions in
her head!

Of her questions, the animals were not a
fan;
they saw her coming, and some just ran!

Why does she do it?
They had to know why.
Then they all thought of a plan
that was sure worth a try.

They'll send Martha to the wise elephant, she'll know
what to do.
She's so full of wisdom and always says what is true!
The animals chose the cheetah to be the one
to tell Martha so that her questions might be done.
But will their plan work?

On *Friday*, Martha caught up with the cheetah running
really fast.
When a question bubbled up, she thought,
I will ask quickly because he won't be the last.
She said, "Hello! It's almost the end of the week,
and I am hoping YOU can give me the answer that I
seek...
Why do you run so fast?"

The cheetah knew just what to say
to quickly get Martha along on her way.
He stated, "I am the fastest animal on Earth, that much
is true.
But asking questions is all that you do!
Please seek out the elephant, she is so wise.
She, too, loves talking and questions,
that's no surprise!"

"Thank you!" said Martha. "You have taught me a lot
and gave me the answer that I have sought!
Toodle-looooo!
Have fun running!"

On *Saturday*, Martha tracked down the elephant
cooling off at the water hole.
When a question bubbled up, she thought,
This is fun! I'm on a roll!
She said, "Hello! It's the end of the week,
and I am hoping YOU can give me the answer that I seek...
Why are you so wise?"

The elephant raised her trunk and began to speak.
But instead of an answer, it was a QUESTION so meek.
"Why do you ask questions each day?
Wouldn't you rather stay out and just play?"

Martha paused... Then her reasons began to overflow.
"There are just so many things that I want to know.
I am curious because I want to learn,
And all my questions begin to burn.
I need to ask them from deep down in my heart
because that is where my knowledge will start.
If I want to be smarter, I can't stay in my tree,
because knowledge is power, as you can plainly see!"

The elephant just smiled when Martha was done.
Then she whispered...

18

Toodle-looooo!
Have fun learning!

Stay curious and be a lifelong learner.

About the Author

Kimberly Hallinan originates from picturesque Central Massachusetts. She continues to reside there with her husband, four children, and grandchildren as well. She is a dedicated and experienced second-grade teacher, as well as a children's author and illustrator who really understands children and how to creatively capture their attention. Kimberly's passion for education shines through her storytelling, and her works inspire young minds to embrace a lifelong journey of learning.

The characters she creates are relevant to the emotional needs and struggles children encounter today. Her writing provides a positive and practical approach to confronting some of these challenges. Through rhyme, rhythm, and repetition, her work provides excellent opportunities to read her stories out loud with those you love.

When she is not teaching, creating, or writing, Kimberly can be found at the ocean, soaking in the sea air and waves; searching for waterfalls; or just seeking an outdoor adventure. She shines her light wherever she goes and loves to leave sparkles behind.

Rooted in faith, this author's love for animals, painting, rhyming, and fun radiates through every page she writes, bringing joy to all those who read her words.